# BY CINDY HELMS

# Outside, Inside

Published by Set Free Publishing ™
Centennial, CO

: § :

*The artwork for each picture and lettering was created with fine art drawing pens and colored pencils. The artwork was scanned into Adobe Photoshop and enhanced for the printed page size.*

*Visit www.CindyHelms.com*

Library of Congress Control Number:  2015906542
Helms, Cindy, Author
Outside, Inside
Cindy Helms

ISBN: 978-0-9963397-0-4

JUVENILE FICTION / Friendship
JUVENILE FICTION / Humorous stories

QUANTITY PURCHASES: Schools, companies, professional groups, clubs, and other organizations may qualify for special terms when ordering quantities of this title. For information, email info@setfreepub.com.

This book is printed in the United States of America.

Centennial, Colorado

For Marshall

inSide.

inSide.

where is everyone today ?

# inSide

ready....

set....

come inSide!

We made this for you

Made in the USA
San Bernardino, CA
03 December 2015